Louise McCloy Horn

Songs of the Lakes and Other Poems

Louise McCloy Horn

Songs of the Lakes and Other Poems

ISBN/EAN: 9783337181871

Printed in Europe, USA, Canada, Australia, Japan

Cover: Foto ©Andreas Hilbeck / pixelio.de

More available books at **www.hansebooks.com**

Songs

OF THE

Lakes

AND OTHER POEMS.

—— BY ——

Louise McCloy Horn.

CINCINNATI
THE EDITOR PUBLISHING CO
1899

INDEX:

SONGS OF THE LAKES.

CRADLE SONGS.

PATRIOTIC SONGS.

RELIGIOUS POEMS.

MISCELLANEOUS.

SONGS OF THE LAKES.

Songs of the Lakes.

LAKE ERIE.

O, tell us, placid waters,
  That stretch away, away,
Tell us the mighty secrets
  Thy bosom holds for aye;
Thou who art old, we pray thee,
  Tell us the wondrous truth—
Thou who dost keep through ages
  The dimples and smiles of youth.

Thou who hast lain unchanging
  A thousand cycles past,
Watching the march of nations
  Each greater than the last;
Nations whose names have perished,
  Buried centuries deep,
And far within thy bosom
  Their records thou dost keep.

O, tell us, cruel waters
  With Heaven's tints abloom,
How many brave and noble
  Have found in thee a tomb?
How many tears of sorrow
  Have swelled thy gleaming waves?
How many hearts have broken
  For those within thy graves?

No word, O, sullen waters,
  Thy gloomy depths will speak;
Thou yieldest not thy knowledge,
  Though that be all we seek;
For if our eyes could search thee
  And read thy hidden lore,
The books of all the ages
  Could never teach us more.

But know, O, silent waters,
  There cometh fast a day
In which thy darkest billows
  Shall all be swept away;
When from thy deepest caverns
  The nameless dead shall rise,
And all the tales of all the years
  Lie clear beneath the skies.

———

SONG OF THE LAKES.

Oh the charm of the dancing waters,
  The rose of the summer morn,
The opal and pearl of the sunsets
  Which pass when the night is born!
I love and I sing of thy glories,
  Ye beautiful inland lakes,
Whether peace reigneth o'er you
  Or whether the tempest breaks.

Away from the din of cities,
  Out where the breezes blow,
Heaven undimmed above you,
  Paths unsullied below.

Here's balm for the heart that's breaking,
　　Here's for the toiler rest.
Here's ease for the brow that's aching,
　　Peace for the care-opprest.

Oh student, turn from your pages;
　　Here is the scroll of truth;
The science and art of Nature
　　Down from the old Earth's youth.
Here's poetry grand in rhythm,
　　Tales for the World to read,
Religion pure from the Maker,
　　Nobler than man-built creed.

Come out on the welcoming waters;
　　'Twill teach you content once more:
Earth's follies and vanities vanish
　　As fadeth the line of the shore.
Let the charm of the waves steal o'er you
　　Which the dusk and the dawn awakes,
The spell of the starry midnights,
　　Till your soul shall sing of the lakes.

———

SUNSET.

We stood upon a bluff out-jutting bold,
　　The turbid waters dashed and broke below—
And watched the cloudless western sky o'erswept
　　By slowly bright'ning beauty till it grew
A glorious, gleaming mass of color rolled
　　From all the Universe.　The sun aglow,
Broad, brilliant, blinding, lower, lower stept;
　　The rolling lake caught on its face a hue
So marvelous our sight could grasp no more
　　And tongues of power to speak it were bereft.

A dye as if the pulsing heart of Time
Eternity's relentless dart had cleft,
And let its blood gush out a-sudden o'er
The heaving world, deep-stained with all its crime.

————

THE SONG OF THE WAVES.

A ceaseless song in mine ear is ringing,
　　The song of the waves;
When the wind of winter their foam is flinging,
When the birds in springtime are northward winging,
Or when, at the time of harvest bringing
　　The lake its rock-wall laves,
I hearken, hush, as I walk anear it
And always, ever, my soul doth hear it.
I love it, weep with it, laugh with it, fear it,
　　The marvelous song of the waves.

Here, where the water is murmuring, crying,—
　　The wail of the waves!
List, it is telling of lovers lying
Down, deep down where no breeze is sighing.
Where sand, slow-shifting, is ever trying
　　To cover their unsought graves.
Heart to heart they went down together;—
Lovers forever, they reck not whether
Fair or foul would have been life's weather;
　　Nothing their slumber craves.

Hear,—by these rocks with the breakers vying,
　　The chant of the waves.
How they are singing of heroes dying
Where death with a thousand bullets flying,
Death, the Dealer. man's life is buying
　　Whose purchase a nation saves.

Now like a wondrous Anthem rolling
Or the roar of a score of iron bells tolling
They raise to the earth a strain consoling,—
    A requiem for its braves.

Hush, where the pines o'er the depths are bending,
    The song of the waves!
A myriad voices are upward sending
Measures of joy and sorrow blending,
Youth and age in a march unending,
    Song of Freemen and song of Slaves.
Love and brightness and woe and wailing
Mingling, changing, swelling and failing
Such is the song my soul assailing;
    The song of the surging waves.

THE LIGHTS ABOVE THE CITY.

On toward the distant city
    Swift the Steamer goes;
Evening breezes rising
    As the darkness grows,
Silver gleaming in her wake,
    Star-lamps shining clear,—
Ah! the lights above the city
    As the boat draws near.

Ah! the lights above the city,
    Lighting many a home;
Throwing rays of welcome
    To the ones who roam.
Lights of peace and plenty
    Lights of warmth and cheer,
The lights above the city
    As the boat draws near.

Ah! the lights above the city,
　They shine on want and woe,
They shine on sin and sorrow
　As the hours of darkness go.
They beam on scenes of revelry
　In hovel and in hall,
They gleam upon the marriage feast
　And on the tear-stained pall.

They shine on wealth and poverty,
　The vilest and the best;
On care that knows no ceasing
　On toil that knows no rest.
On praying and on cursing,
　On love and hate and fear—
The lights above the city
　As the boat draws near.

THE LIFE OF THE SAILOR.

Oh, what is the life of the sailors on the mighty
　　lakes who roam,
　Whose nights and days are on trackless ways,
Who know not the hearths of home;
　Whose sole "good-night" is the star's far light,
Who are kissed at morn by the foam?

Oh, merry the life of the sailor, when waters and
　　winds are fair,
　And happy and glad is the sailor lad,
As his song rings out on the air;
　True-hearted and strong as the day is long,
And his laugh tells naught of care.

And pleasant the life of the sailor when the sun
    comes up in the East,
  When the summer morn is in glory born,
And the white caps foam like yeast;
  When the vibrant steel and the tireless wheel,
Sing praise to their great High-Priest.

But drear is the life of the sailor when sullen and
    dark the sky,
  When the dull swells frown at him gazing down,
And the clouds are gray on high;
  When the wind waits still for the tempest's will,
And the lagging hours go by.

Oh fearful the life of the sailor who the winter's
    wrath must brave,
  When he needs must fight in the cold and night,
The fiends of the wind and wave;
  The hideous foe who would hurl him low,
To an ever-waiting grave.

Aye, this is the life of the sailor; danger and
    toil and pain;
  A heart that cares and a heart that dares
To challenge the treacherous main;
  A heart that sings though the tempest springs,
And laughs, though the storm-king reign.

THE FISHERMAN.

The fisherman, where'er he be,
  Must rise ere break of day.
And when the sun doth dye the sea
  The fleet is far away.
What matter tho' the wind doth blow
  And fiercely flies the foam,
Now high, now low the boat must go,
  While loved ones wait at home.

When dangers ride upon the tide
  The fisher's arm is strong;
When sunny waters dance beside
  His song is loud and long.
For nets must rise when smile the skies
  Or when the tempests roam.
The stout heart flies where duty lies
  When loved ones wait at home.

Ref.

  Then hoist the sail and face the gale
    Tho' wild the morn and drear.
  The fisher's bark is strong and dark,
    The fisher knows no fear.

SONNET. LAKE ERIE ISLANDS.

I know where a nest of Islands lies,
　　Jewel-hued on a bed of blue,
　　Gold of the sunset gleaming through;
They are truant clouds from the summer skies
　　That wandered once when the world was new
(Ah, clouds to-day are far more wise)
Drawn by their own forms' fairy guise
　　In a mirrored sky of the self-same hue.

They floated, lavender, pearl and dove,
　　Gems from the casket of Heaven rare,
And the lake threw around them arms of love
　　And kissed and caressed them lying there,
　　Fairest of all when all was fair,
Nor let them return to their home above.

Cradle Songs.

CRADLE SONG.

Kenneth, my baby, the twilight grows deep,
The soft-stirring leaves hush the robins to sleep,
Hide your brown eyes 'neath their fringed curtains white,
Fold your sweet hands in a dainty good-night.

Kenneth, my baby, no bonnier child
God ever gave mother since Mary's babe smiled.
I dream as I watch thee, my beautiful one,
As a mother-heart ever must dream o'er her son.

What wonder that Israel's mothers of old
Could in such sinless eyes, the Annointed behold!
What wonder the Lord on that long-ago day
Clasped and blessed such as these on the dusty highway.

I wonder as softly beside thee I sing,
What the hastening years to my baby will bring,
What fulfillment will come of a promise so fair,
What the fruitage will be when the bloom is so rare.

Kenneth, my baby, though manhood come soon,
The dawning's soft beauty be lost in the noon,
Though mother thy life to the world must resign—
Thy beautiful babyhood still shall be mine.

And, Oh my heart's treasure, whatever betide
O'er life's pathways untrodden, may God be thy guide;
And when mother's brown hair shall have faded to white,
May her prayers for her son be as glad as to-night.

WHEN EYELIDS DROOP.

Leaning into dreamland
  What does baby see,
Touching thus the curtains
  Of sleep's mystery?
Lingering till the swinging
  Of the slumber-gates,
Past whose silent hinges
  None know what awaits.

Leaning into dreamland
  O'er the walls of sleep—
'Round its low-laid portals
  Dusky shadows creep:
Ever o'er its borders
  Soft clouds hover slow,
Bearing on their bosoms
  Twilight's afterglow.

O'er the dreamland meadows
  Velvet-soft the grass;
Cool and sweet it kisses
  Little feet that pass:
Milky poppies nodding;—
  Daisies meek and fair
Folding their white fingers
  O'er their hearts in prayer.

Leaning into dreamland,—
  See the white lids close,—
Slow, ah slow the gates swing
  As the baby goes.
Dainty mouth a smiling,
  What fair dreams allure?
Sweet must be the visions
  Of a heart so pure.

TO BABY EDNAH.

Baby eyes, browner than Autumn nuts,
  Clearer than stars of night,
Searching the soul's dim corners—
  Darkened and hid from sight:—
Bringing forth to the day-gleam,
  Holding up to our view,
Feelings, fancies and longings
  Solemn and sweet and new.

Baby hands, dimpled and soft and small,
  Sea-shell dainty and fair,
Playing upon our heart-strings
  Melodies deep and rare:
Artists, musicians, sculptors
  Laureled in many lands,
Never can move the nations
  As the touch of a baby's hands.

Baby smiles, soft as the sunshine,
  Flooding the fields in May,
Bringing to flower and fruitage,
  Seeds that are hidden away.
Wakening life to beauty;
  Bidding the mists arise;
Revealing adown dim vistas
  Glimpses of Paradise.

SWEETHEART BOY.

Two small hands remorselessly,
Push the waiting work away:
Two red lips are pressed to mine,
Two plump arms my neck entwine,
While the brownest of brown eyes
Help the soft voice emphasize
  "Kiss a Sweetheart Boy."

Little two-year-old is he,
Filling all the house with glee;
Shouting, laughing at his play,
Into mischief all the day;
Then, when twilight shadows creep,
Pleading—"Mamma, rock to sleep,
  Rock a Sweetheart Boy."

Precious little Sweetheart Boy,
Thy short life has given joy.
More to be desired by far
Than all earthly treasures are.
God and Heaven would nearer be
Could we only learn of thee—
  "Little Sweetheart Boy."

MOTHER GOOSE HOUR.

One in the cradle and one on my knee,
Both are as sleepy as sleepy can be;
Droop the long lashes o'er each drowsy eye
While lips plead, "Sing Blackie-Birds
    Baked in a Pie."

Lower and slower and sleepier too
Comes the petition, "Sing Little Boy Blue."
One is asleep ere the final notes drop,
But the other pleads faintly for,
      "On the Tree-Top."

"Rock-a-bye Baby,"—as leaves of a rose
The red lips are parted with—"When
    the wind blows,"
"When the bough breaks"—how the soft
    breathings fall—
"Down shall come rock-a-bye,
      Baby and all."

AT BEDTIME.

I kissed the crown of her curly head,
    My little maiden of three;—
Her shoulders smooth and her lips so red,
    Her feet and each dimpled knee:
"Now where you found such sweet kisses," I said,
    "Is more than Mamma can see."
From the innocent eyes the laughter fled—
    "Why, God put 'em there when He made me."

CAROL, MY BABY.

Mother kisses your fingers, Precious,
    Kisses them o'er and o'er
And there's born a bliss with each silent kiss
    That's better than all earth's store.
Better than wealth and fame, Precious,
    Better than passion wild,
For naught but the love of God above
    Is as mother's love for her child.

Mother kisses your fingers, Precious,
    Dainty and lily-fair,
And the deeps of your eyes like May time skies
    Are holy as shrines for prayer.
Ah, God is good to us mothers,
    Giving us such as thou,
And looking on thee in thy purity
    We catch the light from His brow.

Mother kisses your fingers, Precious,
    Taught by each lingering kiss
That the luring fires of denied desires
    Are as dross to the gold of this.
I am humble before you, Precious,
    Of such are the Kingdom of Light,
And the path of the soul to its far-off goal
    I see with a plainer sight.

BEDTIME STORIES.

My little girl-birdie is sleepy to-night
    Her brown eyes are tired as can be,
Her feet are a-weary with playing all day
    And she climbs on my welcoming knee.

"Now tell me" she whispers, close nestled and warm,
    " 'Bout once,—Oh a long time ago,
When Mamma was little and lived on a farm
    And slided down hill in the snow.

"N'en tell 'bout the bossies and little white lambs
    And the chickies as cute as can be,
And, Oh Mamma, tell 'bout the tiny round beds
    That the birdies hang up in a tree.

"And please Mamma, tell 'bout the funny brown fish
  That play in the water so deep,
And tell"—but the sweet eyes are hidden at last
  The little girl-birdie's asleep.

TO AZALENE.

Sweetest thy age of all the years,
  Dear little two-year-old.
Each day a pearl from the Heavenly Shore
  Strung on a cord of gold.
Given from God's hand one by one,
  Precious and pure and blest.
At sunset slipping away again
  In the mother's heart to rest.

BABY LORAIN.

Oh, little March Crocus, so fragrant,
  We've a message to tell, sweet and true;
A flower bloomed for us today, Crocus,
  As fair and as dainty as you.

Oh Sunshine, across the floor lying,
  A Sunbeam as pure and as bright
To-day has dropped down out of Heaven,
  And filled all our home with its light.

Oh Bird, singing out in the meadow,
  We have caught from the Beautiful Shore,
A Song from the heart of an Angel,
  To sing in our lives evermore.

Patriotic Songs.

THE SOLDIERS OF OHIO.

Oh, broad and fair Ohio, a hundred years ago
Unbroken were thy solitudes, unchecked thy rivers' flow.
Across thy bosom far and near the solemn forests grew,
And wild and free o'er many a league the winds of winter
   blew.
No prophet dreamed thy destiny, no seer foretold thy fame,
A hundred years seems all too short to build so great a name.

A hundred years, Ohio. and now o'er all the land,
Thy signal-towers of valor on every hill-top stand.
Thy warriors and thy statesmen,—a legion true and brave,
To guard the nation's honor, the nation's name to save—
No other state among us can raise aloft her shield
And show so bright a record upon so fair a field.

Oh, marvelous Ohio, what noble sons are thine;
Hark! rivers of the southland; and list! ye northern pine;
No stronger, grander manhood or North or South can show
Or point to names more honored, where'er the breezes blow.
Aye, thou hast reared, Ohio, thy groves and streams beside,
Men whom the nations reverence with gratitude and pride.

Bear witness, Oh ye battlefields, with christening-cups of
   blood;
Bear witness, Oh ye rivers, that ran with crimson flood,
Bear witness, hills and meadows by cannon rent and torn;
Ohio's sons have through you all Ohio's standard borne;
In camp or march or bivouac, or on the death-swept plain,
Her sword knew not dishonor, her banner knew not stain.

The soldiers of Ohio! Oh may the day ne'er come
When gratitude is wanting, or lips of praise be dumb;
The mothers who have borne them, and trained them duty-
ward,
The wives whose prayers rose daily as incense to the Lord,
Whose hearts kept time to drum-beats, and tears poured
out like rain—
Now let them share the honor as they have shared the pain.

And thou, beloved Ohio, as long as time shall last
May still be found thy record as fair as in the past;
And when the last brave comrade is "mustered out" for aye,
When side by side o'er all the land in silent ranks they lie,
Then may their sons and daughters be still in name and
deed
As brave, as strong, as loyal to serve the nation's need.

OUR ARMY.

Ye boast your standing army, O countries far away,
A million idle soldiers whom starving peasants pay.
A horde who know no service but ceaseless drill and dress,
Learned in the vices of the camp, the lore of idleness.
Your young men, noble Kaiser, and yours, O mighty Czar,
Are brave in lace and uniform, in golden band and star;
Your peasants wear sad faces, your women plow and sow,
And bound in labor's harness the very dogs must go.
Your people know not happiness; they live in hopeless need;
But you boast your standing army which they must toil to
feed.

We have a standing army;—there in the furrowed field
They sow the seed, and gather the harvest's golden yield.
They stand behind the counters, they drive the iron steeds,
At desk or forge or factory they meet a nation's needs.

They know the sweets of labor, they eat the bread of toil,
Across the mighty land they reach, where e'er is freedom's
    soil;
But let one voice demand them, let but one drum-beat fall—
From out a million happy homes they answer to the call:
No star upon our banner but makes its quota good;
And rich and poor and black and white know naught but
    brotherhood.

————

MEMORIAL DAY.

Yes, we are thoughtless, you and I,
    Selfish and thoughtless and know it not;
The thievish years as they hasten by
    Have blinded our eyes and seared our heart.

In what are we selfish? In this, my Friend,
    That we sit at rest in our pleasant land,
Where power and liberty meet and blend,
    Wrapped in a peace which is royal, grand.

And we give no thought to the souls that fled
    Thousands on thousands that peace to buy:
We give no thought to the hearts that bled;
    Bled and broke to see dear ones die.

Scarcely the sounds of their drums has died,
    The echo of marching feet grown still;
Scarcely the stain of their blood has dried
    O'er a thousand miles of meadow and hill.

And we, their kindred, with careless hand
    Reap the blessings they fought and won,
And all too seldom our hearts expand
    For those who slumber, their life-work done.

We cannot pay them the debt we owe;
  Can we pay our God for the care he gives?
Can we pay for a Mother's love?   Ah, no.
  Such debts are debts while the debtor lives.

So our soldier martyrs we cannot pay;
  Earth has no coin for a work so great,
But our gratitude can be theirs for aye,
  And honor and love on their memory wait.

And ever as passing years shall bring
  The day to their memory set apart,
May blossoms of love and thankfulness spring
  In the garden-ground of each loyal heart.

And when, in a far off day unknown
  Our country is called no longer young,
But mightier far and wiser grown,
  Still by its sons may their praise be sung.

———

THEY HAVE STRUCK THEIR TENTS.

The strife is over, the years have fled;
The grasses cover the slumbering dead;
Peaceful and fair beneath the sky
The battlefields and the trenches lie;
Silent and grim each black-mouthed gun
Since the tents were struck when the war was done.

Many a spring with its gold and green
North and Southland alike have seen
Since a host, triumphant, marched once more
Back to the North and the homestead door,
Leaving a host, both Blue and Gray,
Who had struck their tents till the Judgment Day.

No more die men by a brother's hand,
Please God forever, in our fair land,
But fast, ah fast do the soldiers fall
By the grim sharpshooter who waits for all;
Each day for some are life's battles done,
And they strike their tents, aye, one by one.

Steadily, steadily, day by day,
Is the great host marching away, away.
They hark to the signal more and more,
"Fall in, fall in," for another shore;
And they strike their tents in the morning light
And pass forever from earthly sight.

But though they go from this land of ours
To the still, green beds which we deck with flowers,
Though the blue-clad columns year by year
In slower, thinner ranks appear
Yet never, never, though we part,
Will they strike their tents in the nation's heart.

And comrades, brothers who dared to go
In the name of Freedom to face the foe—
When you're "mustered out" at the last roll-call,
"Discharged with honor" be each and all:
May they answer gladly where e'er they roam
When the tents are struck and the "boys" go home.

THE PASSING HOST.

Across the midnight sky it lies,
 Far-reaching, vast and grand,
The unsolved mystery of the skies
 O'er every sea and land!

The milky way. The darkness shows
　　Its wond'rous notes and bars:
A heavenly score which pales and glows
　　While sing the morning stars.

It lends the gloomy dome of night
　　Its beauty and its grace;
And scatters radiance and light
　　On every land and race.

But when the dim faint tints of morn
　　Foretell the coming day,
'Ere yet within the east is born,
　　The first resplendent ray,

Then swift, ah, swift, its glory goes,
　　Its marvels disappear;
Its radiance fainter, fainter grows,
　　And dawning day draws near,

*　　　*　　　*　　　*　　　*

E'en thus across our country's sky,
　　When sudden darkness fell,
When hearts grew faint at dangers nigh,
　　And none the way could tell,

There flashed a radiance far and near,
　　A myriad stars aglow,
Blending and gleaming fair and clear,
　　A host no man might know.

Heroic souls who fainted not,
　　Strong hearts that would not fail,
Brave eyes that watched while others fought;
　　Fair faces, sad and pale.

They made the darkness glorious,
  They pierced the deepest night,
They spoke a cause victorious,
  The triumph of the right.

The midnight passed and one by one
  We watched them fade and die;
And as they go, may night be done
  And dawning day draw nigh.

Aye, those that struggled, those that wept,
  Through hours of doubt and fear,
In silence from our sight are swept;
  And, lo! the morn is here.

A new, grand morn for all the world,
  The Twentieth Century;
May earth with every flag unfurled
  Salute it in the sky. .

And thou, oh God of war and peace,
  While nations rise and fall,
Haste now the day when strife shall cease.
  And love shine over all.

GREETINGS TO THE VETERANS.

Once in a far-off country,
  When, after a conquest grand,
The King and his hosts came marching
  Home to the fatherland,
As they neared the gates of the city
  The watchman upon the wall
With trumpets summoned the people
  Eagerly waiting the call.

Then out they thronged from the cottage,
  And out from the palace gay,
To welcome with shouts and music
  The army from far away.
Cheer after cheer re-echoed
  As the weary soldiers came
Marked with the stains of warfare,
  Footman and horse the same.

Cheers for the guarded captives,
  Sullen irom fear and pain:
Cheers for the spoils of conquest
  Borne in a long-drawn train.
But hush! And the cheers are silent;
  What do the heralds call?
They come! The King and his legion,—
  The bravest and best of all!

Then the people bend in reverence
  With never a cheer nor cry,
And the silence is deep and solemn
  While the King is passing by.
Cheers are for all the others,—
  Glad do the echoes ring,—
But silence, only silence
  For the legion of the King.

And thus we stand, O Veteran,
  Before you here to-day.
Our lips but poorly fashion
  The thoughts our hearts would say.
For words, oft-times so mighty,
  Are weak and faltering now
And silence seems most fitting
  In greeting such as thou.

We think of homes made desolate,
  Of loving hearts that broke,
Of lives laid down by thousands
  Amid the battle-smoke;
Of suffering unfathomed
  In prison-pen and field,
Of cold and hunger;—hearts that bled
  But knew not how to yield.

We think of what we owe to thee:—
  A broad and glorious land,
In peace and liberty unmatched,
  In union strong and grand;
Which fears no foe; which floats a flag
  Beloved on every sea;
With homes secure 'mid fruitful fields,—
  All this we owe to thee.

And so, with hearts which seek in vain
  For fitting words, we bow:
The whole wide country greeteth thee
  With silent reverence now:
And while the stars and stripes shall wave,
  Their voiceless speech shall be,
On whatsoever sea or shore,
  A greeting unto thee.

DECORATION DAY.

Echoing over the land to-day,
By the sands of the ocean dying away,
A thousand voices in word and song
Mourn for the fallen, mourn for the strong.
A thousand hands lay the May-time bloom
Over the sleeping soldiers' tomb,
And thousands think of the graves that lie
Unknown, unhonored beneath the sky.

Thirty years have the light and shade
Over their resting-places played;
Thirty years since the war-cloud broke,
Thirty years since the echoes woke:
And ten times thirty shall circle round
And still shall the pulsing echoes sound,
And names shall live as the years roll on
As liveth the name of Marathon.

Thirty years o'er the blood-drenched plains
Have fallen the mournful Autumn rains;
Thirty springs o'er the war-scarred hills
Have wafted the breath of daffodils,
But shower nor blossom nor waving grain
Never can blot out Gettysburg's stain,
Nor the storms of a thousand years erase
The path to the sea that Sherman traced.

To-day how memory wakes to life
In the breasts of those who watched the strife,
Whether under the Southern skies
Seeing the battle-smoke arise,
Or under the milder Northern sun
Where the heart's fierce battles were lost or won;
Matrons to-day, and gray-haired men—
They were but youths and maidens then.

Again they hear across the years
The country's call for volunteers,
And feel once more the awful thrill
That heralded the Nation's ill.
Again as the rolling drum·beat falls
'They hear the shout o'er Sumpter's walls,
Or see the first warm life-blood pour
In the crowded streets of Baltimore.

A thousand veterans fight anew
Shiloh and Fair Oaks of '62.
See Chickamauga's blood-stained breast
Or gaze on Lookout's cloud-capped crest.
Rebel prisons their scenes unfold,
Weary marches, hunger and cold,
The cheer of the camp, the game, the song,
And all that to soldiers' lives belong.

But cometh the day when none shall say
"Do you remember"—of Blue or Gray.
Cometh the day when far or near
None to the roll-call answer "here."
Cometh the day and cometh fast
When the last of the thinning ranks has passed
And a legion lie 'neath the blooms of May
Who follow the beating drums to-day.

But not the least of the battles fought,
Not the least of the great deeds wrought
Were done afar from the scenes of strife
Afar from the sound of drum and fife.
Were done by wives, by daughters fair,
By suffering mothers everywhere,
Who, knowing not Gethsemane's gloom,
Gethsemane find at the cross and tomb.

The crowd of the martyr they may not bear
The vestments of honor they may not wear,
No roster ever hath borne their name;
They hold no rank in the lists of fame,
But on Freedom's Altar they feed the blaze
As the Vestal Virgins in Rome's great days,
And a mighty debt to their hearts and hands
In the Nation's unread record stands.

And soldiers, sleeping beneath the dew
Or wearing still the Army Blue,
All honor to thy deed and name,
Whate'er thy rank, whate'er thy fame,
For deeds shall live though brows lie cold
And memories fade to legends old.
And Freedom aye shall deck thy tombs
With gratitude's unfading blooms.

Religious Poems.

UNTO THE HILLS.

"Unto the hills from whence cometh our strength,"
Grandly the chorus of Israel thrills.
Small wonder, O Psalmist, the wings of thy music,
Carried thy soul like a bird to the hills.

"I will lift up mine eyes," so the melody ringeth,
Away from earth's trials, and struggles, and sin,
Unto the hills where the Father's hand resteth,
Emblems of strength that is mighty to win.

Unto the hills never failing and peaceful;
Firm 'mid the tempest through ages untold;
Millions the feet which their pathways have trodden;
Millions the graves which their bosoms enfold.

"From whence cometh our strength," O Creator and **Father,**
Thou in whose might earth's high places can trust,
Thou, and Thou only, our need of strength knoweth,
Who remembereth that we, like the mountains, are dust.

Strength for life's daily temptations and trials;
Strength to be patient with friend as with foe;
Strength for Thy charity, strength for forgiving,
As we Thy forgiveness, O Father would know.

Strength to live strongly and nobly before Thee,
Hast'ning Thy kingdom with labor and prayer,
Humble with sense of our guilt and our weakness,
Strong in Thy strength and secure in Thy care.

Unto the hills in their grandeur and beauty,
Lovingly, trustingly, lift we our eyes,
Thanksgiving and praise from earth's hilltops, O Father,
Forever like incense to Thee shall arise.

THE BENEDICTION.

We stood before him with bended heads
  In the hush of the Sabbath, with one accord.
"And now may you grow in Grace," he said,
  "And in knowledge and love of Christ, our Lord."

The music echoed from dome and wall
  Drowning the greeting and low-voiced word,
And throbbing and murmuring through it all
  Over and over again I heard—

"Grow in Grace"—how the echoes rang!
  "And in knowledge and love, O Christ, of Thee."
Till the chords of my heart responsive sang,
  And a prayer rose out of the melody.

"Oh Master, Thou with a voice so winning,
  Love and peace in Thine eyes divine,
Help us, willful and blind and sinning,
  That down on our hearts Thy light may shine.

For a greater change than the Springtime maketh
  Earth and its suffering hosts shall know.
When the light of life in each heart awaketh
  And in love and knowledge of Thee we grow.

"Grow in Grace," O our Lord and Master,
  Haste, we pray Thee, the blessed day,
When truth and righteousness, fast and faster
  Banish hatred and greed away.

When knowledge of Thee shall be richest treasure,
Sought as men seek for gold and fame.
And our lives shall grow to their grandest measure,
In grace and love of Thy wondrous Name.

NO OTHER NAME.

Lying for alms at the Beautiful Gate
Helpless and maimed did the lame man wait;
Daily the worshipers passed him by,
Fleet and active, eager of eye.
Daily of pity and alms they gave,
But none of the throng could help or save.

Naught did he know of the city's strife,
Naught did he know of the flow of life.
Joy of boyhood and youth's warm zeal,
Strength of manhood, he ne'er could feel:
Hopelessly, wearily, life's drear day —
Morning and noontide, passed away.

Came there two on that long gone day—
Plain in raiment and poor were they—
But none of the stately Pharisees bore
On face or figure the grace they wore—
Strength and wisdom and love and rest —
Peter, forgiven, and John the Blest.

"Silver and gold have I none" said he,
"But such as I have will I give unto thee.
In the name of the Christ who from Nazareth came,
Rise up and walk." Ah, the wonderful Name!
He lifted the maimed one, hand in hand,
And over him flooded a life-tide grand.

On the morrow they questioned them, rulers grave,
Elders and priests, "By what power to save,
By what marvelous Name did ye this thing do?"
List to the words to eternity true!
"There is no other Name among men known,
Able to save us, but Christ's alone."

No other Name, oh, sin-maimed earth,
Helpless and suffering, lame from birth;
No other Name, oh, ye who lie
Crushed and trampled, ready to die.
No other Name; but humanity's woes
Christ, the tempted and crucified, knows.

Hopeless, ye sit at the Beautiful Gate;
Naught do ye know of the joys that wait.
Bowed 'neath thy burden beside the way.
Falling and perishing day by day.
No other name beneath the skies,
But the Name of the Christ can bid thee rise.

CHRISTIAN ENDEAVOR.

Let us broaden our hearts, O Brothers;
　Let love grow up in our souls
Till over the whole, wide, suffering earth,
　The tidal wave, Charity, rolls.

Let us scorn not humanity, Brothers;
　Out of Nazareth cometh the Christ,
For the lowly, the sinful, the weary,
　Were his glory and life sacrificed.

Let us rise above selfishness, Brothers;
　Round us heaven showers its store.
There are many on earth who have nothing,
　Can their poverty be at our door?

Aye, many and many, My Brothers,
  Born to suffering, wretchedness, shame.
Oh can we not reach them and help them,
  In His love and the power of His name?

"To the least of these," think, O My Brothers;
  We living for self and for friend,
To our ears is the "Inasmuch" coming,
  When life shall have rounded the end!

Then low at the feet of the Master,
  In love and in shame let us bow;
The world Thou hast died for, Our Saviour,
  O, help us to live for it now.

POST TENEBRAS LUX.

Through the valleys slowly wending,
Hope and doubt forever blending,
Prayer for guidance upward sending,
  We await the dawning day.
Through the darkness piercing never,
Held by bonds we cannot sever,
Still out-reaching, striving ever,
  We are guided on our way.

Woe and gladness mingled meet us,
Voice of foe and lover greet us,
Upward still the pathways lead us,
  On to joy and peace and rest.
Weary hands shall soon be light,
Mortal vision dim grow bright,
Waiting hearts shall see aright,
  Freedom come to souls opprest.

Though the pathway be but drear,
See! the hill-tops grow more clear,
Draweth now the dawning near,
    Heart, look upward, onward press.
Still the beck'ning hand pursue,
Failing strength again renew,
Power will come to be and do,
    Soon we'll wear immortal dress.

And at last the journey ending,
We, the mountain-tops ascending
View the day-break glories blending
    With the scattering shades of night.
Free from all the chains that bound us,
Free from all the shadows round us,
Soon the sunrise shall have found us,—
    After darkness comes the light.

CHILDREN OF GOD.

Call us not servants, Lord, we pray,
But children, often led astray;
Children who love, but disobey.

Who wander, while the sun is bright,
Far from a loving Father's sight,
But haste to him when nears the night.

Who, heedless, till the day has fled
Have loitered where their fancy led,
Then look to Thee for daily bread.

Call us not servants, is our prayer,
Children, who crave thy constant care,
Thy tenderness beyond compare.

Who would thy will should shape their deeds,
But know an Elder Brother pleads
For each frail child that pardon needs.

OUR DWELLING PLACE.

After the toil of the day and its trials,
Life's disappointments, hope's constant denials.
After the efforts that ended in failing,
After the laughter whose echo was wailing,
After the seeking that never is finding,
After the pathway so rough and so winding.
Wayworn and weak with our wearisome roaming,
Turn we at last in the star-lighted gloaming
 Home to onr Dwelling Place, Father, in Thee.

Fortress art Thou, sin's besiegers defying.
Beautiful Palace, heart's longings supplying,
Refuge, with enemy never molesting,
Home for the weary, with loving and resting,
Altar that satisfies all the soul's yearning,
School, with no end to its wonderful learning,
Down through all ages, in all generations
Up from the deeps of earth struggle the Nations
 Seeking their Dwelling Place, Father, in Thee.

SATISFIED.

Oh, the hungry, longing Soul,
 As the solemn ages roll
Seeketh ever, seeketh ever, somewhere to abide.
 Seeketh food and shelter meet,
 Seeketh friends and converse sweet,
Seeketh pleasant waters with meadows green beside.

Every age and every clime
Since the sunny morn of Time
Has the Soul, blindfolded, wandered far and wide.
Treading sad and weary
Deserts wide and dreary,
Feeding, royal prodigal, on husks for swine supplied.

Building temples treasure-trove
To Mahomet, Buddha, Jove,
Finding not in all its quest the God for which it cried.
Finding refuge never,
Dread and darkness ever,
Sorrow, toil and anguish, death and naught beside.

Haste, oh haste the glorious dawn
Of the long-awaited morn
When the Soul, returning, seeks its Father's side.
Haste, Oh God, the day supernal
When we, through Thy love eternal,
In Thy likeness waking, shall be satisfied.

----

*A QUARTER CENTURY.

As out-bound sailors turn to view
the fast receding shore,
Or pilgrims up the mountain-side,
gaze back the pathway o'er,
E'en thus our steps have halted, to
scan the path we tread—
A quarter-century behind,
Eternity, ahead.
A quarter-century of toil, of faith
and hope and pain;
A quarter-century of love,
of blessing and of gain,

* Read at the twenty-fifth anniversary of the founding of a church.

Of deeds imprinted by the stern
    Recording Angel's hand,
Of words, perchance, which may not die,
    while earthly hilltops stand.
For who can weigh the value of
    prayers and hopes and tears,
Or measure out the fruitfulness
    of five and twenty years?
Aye, as the May-flower started,
    that morning long ago,
Deep-freighted with what issues,
    the Lord alone could know,
So starts each band that ventures
    across Time's unknown sea,
"Thy Kingdom Come," their watch-word,
    their port, Eternity.
No nobler work, O Brothers,
    can human hands essay,
Than in the Master's service
    to labor day by day.
No other field so mighty, no other
    end so sure,
No other fruits so glorious,
    so certain to endure.
No other life so happy, so peaceful
    and so blest,
No other pathway leading on
    to God's eternal rest.
Who knows what feet within these walls
    to straighter paths have turned?
Who knows what hearts beneath this roof
    with purer thoughts have burned?
Who knows what waves of blessing, have
    started from this door,
Forever widening onward to Heaven's
    unchanging shore?

With thankful hearts we gather
in this His temple, now;
With humblest gratitude and love,
before His throne we bow;
To Him who thus hath led us, and
blest us on the way,
Whose grace has been our sure defence,
whose love has been our stay.
Whose mercy and whose tenderness
are an unfailing store,
To Him be love and service, and
praise forevermore.
And yet, what heart but saddens,
at thought of good undone?
Of anger unforgiven at setting of
the sun?
Of suffering unlightened,
Of prison doors unsought?
Defeat instead of victory in many
battles fought?
Of judgment for the erring,
instead of loving aid?
Of halting feet which often from
narrow paths have strayed?
God give us strength and wisdom;
God teach our hearts to see
The beauty of unselfishness,
The joy of ministry.
God broaden out our vision,
that we may feel indeed
The pleadings of humanity,
the world's unfathomed need;
That we may know ourselves sent out,
as Christ was sent of old,
And hear him saying,"Feed my lambs,"
and bring them to the fold.

God teach our hearts to covet
 His wondrous gifts in store,
Till earthly wealth and honor,
 shall tempt us nevermore.
God guide us in his service
 till all at last shall know,
The peace which consecration
 can on our hearts bestow;
And when at last is finished
 for each this earthly race,
And from His church below we rise
 to see the Master's face,
With strivings all behind us,
 life's toilsome journey run,
O Father, Master, may we hear
 thine accents say, "Well done."

———

STEWARDSHIP.

Thou hast said, O Lord, that the earth is thine,
The earth and its fullness are thine alone.
Yet we hoard and keep what is not our own,
And say in our hearts. "All this is mine."
Forgive us, Lord, that thy children die—
Starve and die in a broad, fair land,
Perish daily in reach of our hand,
And we on the other side pass by.
Nay, more; so long have our eyes been blind,
So long is our Stewardship forgot,
Though the cries are legion we hear them not,
Nor think that our hand should the death-wound bind.
O, master, forgive, that thy name we bear,
But thy garment of pity we do not wear.

MUMMIES.

We're mummies, friend, we're mummies, I say,
Deep under Pyramids hidden away,
The sun cannot pierce the stones that rise
Heavy and damp above one's eyes,
And wandering breezes perfumed rare
Never can touch one's brow or hair.

Mummies embalmed with myrrh and spice,
And bitter aloes of selfishness;
Wound and bound with fold on fold
Of creeds and dogmas and doctrines old,
In a coffin of orthodoxy strong
Slumbering peacefully, sound and long.

The stones above us are massive and cold,
Cut from the quarries old, so old,
Of the World's Opinions, which first and last,
Are found in the heart of the hill of Caste.
The rivers of Mammon flow close beside
And empty into the gulf of Pride.

Perhaps you remember the corn that lay
In the tomb of Pharaoh stored away: —
Think you the germ had started green
In the thousand years since the grain was seen?
Seeds in creeds may be good, I know,
But they need the sunlight before they'll grow.

The sunlight of Love falls warm from the sky
And life is only obtained thereby.
Like Moses' rod, where the sunbeams knock,
Life's water will flow from the solid rock,
And the heart where love shines full and free
A very fountain of youth shall be.

Mummies, I said; nay tranced instead,
And we may, if we will, arise and shed
Each blinding bandage, each fold unroll
Till the sunlight falls on the darkened soul;
And small and slight will the Pyramids be
Compared with the height of a soul set free.

—— ——

PATIENCE.

Often, when night and its quiet falls around you,
When, after day's failures, the rest-time has found you,
    Life's slow-yielding vineyards you scan,
Look up to the sky softly over you leaning,
And draw from its grandeur the clear written meaning
    Of the Maker who careth for man.

Patiently labor; all round us is beauty:
Lilies bloom ever where runs the path Duty,
    Lilies with hearts filled with dew.
If your sun seems to set, life's light seems to fail,
Cometh not with the darkness the sweet nightingale?
    The starlight soft-fingered and true?

Labor for others; thy life He is molding;
Ever thy times in his hands He is holding;
    He giveth the drops as they fall.
Then wait, though the waiting be never so dreary;
Only to God is thy life rounded clearly:
    He knoweth the ending of all.

Fate, born of God's thought, can never miscarry;
Man cannot force it to haste or to tarry:
    Be patient and wait for His will.
Ah, well for His children who chafe at His leading,
Who spurn the cool pastures wherein they are feeding,
    That He who is love, loveth still.

REVELATION.

A lightning flash in the night,
  An instant and then it is o'er:
What a revelation of light
  Where nothing was seen before!
The dew-wet grass at your feet.
  The twigs of the beech tree there,
Blossoms and leaves complete
  Etched in the sapphire air.

A lightning flash in the night:
  So, sometimes, O heart of mine,
There flashes a wondrous light
  O'er those night-wrapped eyes of thine;
And they see in that moment's sight
  How sinful and black thou art
To a God as pure as the light:—
  And thou bowest in shame, O heart.

Thou seest aghast where hate,
  Malice and vanity thrive,
Where envy and jealousy mate,
  And evil is kept alive.
Thou seest a life that bears
  The name of the Christ in vain;
A mantle of selfishness wears
  And strives for pleasure and gain.

A lightning flash in the night:
  So, sometimes, out of thy trance,
My soul, thou wakest to sight
  And knoweth thine ignorance.
There flashes a concept dim
  Of the infinite depths of Space,
Unthinkable save to him
  Who watches their chariot-race.

Thou catchest an instant's gleam
 ·Of the Universe of God,
Where a million worlds unseen
 Swing in their circles broad;
The awfulness of the years
 Weighing thee down, O Soul,
Thou shrinkest with sudden fears,
 With dread thou canst not control.

ANNIVERSARY HYMN.

[TUNE:—Portuguese Hymn.]

Our hearts rise to Thee, Oh our Father above,
 In grateful remembrance of mercy and love,
Thine hand hath upheld us, thine arm been our stay,
 Thy strength and thy Spirit have guided our way.

We thank Thee, we praise Thee with service and song:
 Our hearts and our voices to Thee do belong.
Our prayers would rise ever in loving accord
 To Him who hath saved us, through Jesus our Lord.

Oh, lead us, and help us, and cause us to know
 Thy will and thy wishes as onward we go,
Thy kingdom to hasten our aim in the fight,
Thy service our pleasure, thy way our delight.

Miscellaneous.

THE DYING POET.

The sunset lit the land and sea;
  The quiet deepened round him;
We would not break by word or touch
  The Sabbath-peace that bound him.

The radiance broadened in the West;
  The sea was opal-gleaming;
The poet murmured as he lay
  As children do in dreaming.

And softly did the breathed words
  Drop into sudden rhyming
Like bells of long-gone Christmases
  O'er moonlit meadows chiming,

In thought he was a child again, —
  His mother's voice a-calling,
And on his brow at eventide
  Soft, sudden kisses falling.

The lengthening shadows eastward fell:
  The crimson clouds slow drifted;
Through interlacing maple boughs
  The dazzling light was sifted.

Again the measured murmurs rose; —
  His boyhood passed before him;
Around him were the fields and hills,
  The skies of youth shone o'er him.

44

The crimson West to purple turned;—
The words fell low and tender;—
A maiden's love-lit eyes he saw,
He clasped warm fingers slender.

The sea grew gray. From distant hills
The radiance faded slowly.
The poet's voice to silence died;
The room was hushed and holy.

Thicker the shades around us fell;
His breath came slow and slower:
The golden gleams upon the West
Grew dimmer still and lower.

We bent above the peaceful face,
Love's tender smile still wearing.
Far in the sky the drifting clouds
Day's last, faint gleam were bearing.

We knew on other, fairer lands
The sunrise light was breaking.
To life and love the poet's soul
Beyond the sun was waking.

JUNE.

To the lyre, O Apollo! June cometh again;
Sound her praises abroad to the children of men.
Regal June! Straight from Heaven her pathway she takes.
O'er the earth's pulsing heart her sweet censer she shakes.

O beauty, awaken! O perfume arise!
O birds, sound your choral beneath the far skies!
Life is fair, O Queen June, with thy sceptre awave;
Earth has turned to a bridal instead of a grave.

O ye barriers finite, the angel-bands throng
So close to thy portals we catch their far song,
And the air is a-tremble with ecstacy deep,
For the spirit of love has awakened from sleep.

The flower-bells are ringing their anthems of praise,
The leaves of the forest their glad chorus raise;
All nature has marshaled her forces in tune,
To the Giver of beauty, the Giver of June.

Lift your eyes, O humanity, see and rejoice;
Let your gladness thrill out from your hearts through your
      voice;
Let the pæan of thankfulness heavenward roll;
From the midst of His love, praise the Lord, O my soul!

COBWEBS.

Over and over within my mind,
      Back from a childhood golden,
A picture comes of a volume worn,
Coverless, dog-eared, battered and torn,
Sacred 'mongst juvenile treasurers borne,
      "Mother Goose Melodies" olden.

Folly of follies, we think, and smile,
      Recalling its childish fancies;
And yet, perchance, it is better far
Than many weightier volumes are;
No harmful teachings its pages mar,
      No evil its charm enhances.

One pictured tale I remember well,
      As o'er them memory lingers,
About the old woman who flew so high
To sweep the cobwebs out of the sky,
With pointed cap and her hair awry,
      And a worn old broom in her fingers.

Childish and foolish the little rhyme:
    Yet often the thought arises
That under the folly there still may be
A lesson lying for you and me,
For deepest truths we may sometimes see
    Under most strange disguises.

How many a grave reformer now,
    In this, the age of reformers,
With vigorous broom and piercing eye
Is trying to cleanse the whole wide sky
Of dusty webs that he claims to spy
    In all of its distant corners!

And are we not prone, in a narrower way
    To think our efforts are needed
To sweep some particular spot of blue,
Where we fancy the light does not shine through
With all the power it were equal to
    If only its course were heeded?

Ah, let us come down to our own small lives,
    Down to our own heart's chambers,
Use our brooms on the cobwebs here,
Then when the walls are swept and clear
We'll have better right to interfere
    With the cobwebs blinding our neighbors.

But I think ere our task is done we'll say,
    If we give our honest opinions,
That life is too short and our strength too small,
To leave us any leisure at all
For sweeping down cobwebs large or small
    Outside of our own dominions.

DEAD—AGED 26.

"THE END IS VISION."

And so the problem's solved,—solved easily, -
As other problems are, by the Master's touch.
How simple the equation in the light
Of this solution,—so abstruse before.
The blame, the strife, the hurt, the scanty praise,—
Too scanty far for the love-yearning heart—
The clipping wings to bring to earthly use
A creature not of earth—how vain is all
In view of this,—the problem perfected
And death, not life, the unknown quantity.
    "What use," he always said, "this money-strife,
This search for knowledge,—wisdom of the world?"
What use indeed, with Heaven ahead, not earth!
Back-gazing o'er the life we blamed so much
For lacking earthly purpose, how the words
Of one—another youth—come, "Wist ye not,"
To chiding Mother, "I must be about
My Father's business?" Ah, Mary blamed, and yet
She had the angels' message. We had none.
And, after all, the blame grew out of love
With her and us. Blind-folded human love.
We'd be no wiser for more messages.
Some lives there are whose work on earth is more
To be than do. Eternity shows fruit.
And now the flowers, the perfume,—heavy, rich,—
The music, eulogy,—love-prompted—all.
I wonder how they look—these things—to a soul
Three days in Heaven. All the grief, remorse,
The agony—to eyes now opened clear
To the largeness of God's plan. Each reason plain
For every step so erstwhile purposeless.

The straightness of His leadings—Ah, my friend,
That's where we fail,—that's where the blindness comes:
His plan—His leadings,—we would wrest away
As petulant children from the father-hand
And live our lives and guide our children's lives
By our own small wisdom's measure,—plan for earth,
While He plans for Eternity and Heaven.
Life's bitterness and pain—how small 'twould grow
If but His children knew the guiding hand
For all alike, and heard the voice—"Lo! I
Am with you always, even to the End."

THE CROWN-BIRD.

Back in the days of fable
  When this old earth was young,
When nature throbbed with music
  And every thought was sung;
When Clotho's shining distaff
  Spun out the threads of life,
And Jove from high Olympus
  Looked down on peace or strife:

There flew, o'er beauteous Hellas,
  —So saith the fable old—
A wondrous bird, broad-breasted
  With pinions strong and bold.
And whom those pinions shadowed,
  From ether circling down,
High-born were he or lowly,
  His head should wear a crown.

Mayhap some humble shepherd
  In Thracian meadows wide
His loitering flock drives homeward
  As nears the eventide;

If o'er his eyes up-gazing
  The bird's dark shadow falls,
He sees his peaceful pastures
  Change into royal halls.

Or if some youthful Mother
  Her sleeping babe should place
Where wandering breezes whisper
  And blossoms touch his face,
And o'er his head unheeding
  Should soar the shadowing wings,
Then for the tiny sleeper
  Awaited robes of kings.

Earth's sordid aims have silenced
  The music of her youth;
Eyes have grown blind to beauty,
  Ears have grown dull to truth;
Perchance, could we but see it,
  Still does the crown-bird soar,
And shadow brows crown-fated
  As said the Greeks of yore.

THE OLD GARRET ROOM.

Of the perfumes of Araby poets may sing,
  Of tropic isles spicy and warm,
But the breath of the Orient can not compare
  With the old Garret Room on the farm.
Where the rafters sloped down to the swallow-swept eaves,
  And the wasp masons never knew harm,
And the architect–spiders built palaces vast,
  In the old garret room on the farm.

Where the bunches of catnip were hung by a string,
  With spearmint and peppermint near,

And the sage swung aloft in a spicy repose
  Till the thanksgiving turkey appear.
The burdock and yellow dock bided their time,
  By their side did the dandelion swing;
For they knew that a sure resurrection would come
  When the "bitters" were made in the Spring.

The tansy and carraway mingled their scents
  With the hops and the withered sweet-flag,
And the red-clover blooms a drear prison had found
  In a dusty and dark paper bag.
There a coverless coffee-pot stood on a ledge,
  And, deep in its gloomy recesses,
Were packets of seeds of a goodly old age—
  Sweet Williams and string-beans and lettuce.

Aye, poets may sing of the vales of the East,
  Of rose-gardens spicy and sweet,
But never a vale or a garden, I know,
  With the old garret room can compete.
The old garret room with its dust and its gloom,
  Its atmosphere heavy and warm,
Its age-blackened rafters hung thickly with herbs—
  The old garret room on the farm.

IRELAND.

Oh Ireland, thou child of Utopian birth,
How camest thou here in this wearisome earth!
So far out of step in humanity's strife,
So illy equipped for the struggle of life.
What pleasure hast thou in this world's bitter wine,
Whose faults are all virtues, whose virtues divine?
The one spot art thou in this dreary world wide,
Where the serpent, the symbol of sin, can not hide.

The muses, of whom but faint glimpses we catch,
Take up their abode beneath thy humble thatch,
And song springs as free from the lips and the hearts,
As thy shamrock in Spring from the green hillside starts.
Mirth and gladness are thine though the heart break the
　　　while,
For smiles gleam through tears in the Emerald Isle;
But, Erin, thy leaven the world's bread doth need,
And bereft of thy lightness 'twere heavy indeed.

Our bravest in battle as sons thou canst claim;
They fill the front ranks in the long roll of Fame;
Their speech falleth golden from Eloquence' height
As the star-flames of Venus pierce down through the night.
Is there need of their bounty, their all they bestow,
Though the morrow yield harvest of hunger and woe;
Nor can billows of pain or of poverty part
The smile from the lip, or the song from the heart.

OVER ON THE CROSS-ROAD.

Over on the cross-road,
　　Years and years ago,
Lay a land enchanted,
　　None of us might know;
When the old red school-house
　　Stood upon the hill,
Just beyond the graveyard,
　　Ever cool and still.

Over on the cross-road
　　Black-berries grew wild,
Nodding through the rail fence,
　　When I was a child.

In the stony pastures
  Grew the mullein white;
Browsed the sheep in day-time,
  Piped the quail at night.

Over on the cross-road
  Stretching far away,
Lost at last to vision
  In the woodland gray—
Sometimes came a peddler,
  Bending neath his load;
Or a dusty beggar,
  Loitering up the road.

When the twilight settled,—
  Stars came out above,—
Somewhere down the cross-road
  Grieved the mourning dove.
Then the ghostly wild-fire
  Gleamed and died away,
And the bare-foot urchins
  Shivered at their play.

Time brings disenchantment,
  But we think of thee
O, thou country cross-road
  Wrapped in mystery!
As life's many cross-roads
  Through the years appear,
All their glamor losing,
  As we draw more near.

A DEAD HOPE.

Through the sunshine and shadow adown the still street,
O'er arched by the elm boughs which sigh as they meet
A flutter of crape from a cottage door tells
That within those home-walls grief unspeakable dwells.
We know that a loved one lies robed for the grave,
And heart touches heart as the sad emblems wave;
For bereavement makes brotherhood all the world o'er,
And humanity bows to the crape on the door.

But ah, when a pure hope is born in the heart,
Growing daily to be of its life-force a part,
Lending strength to each prayer, to each smile giving grace,
Making sweeter the voice and more gentle the face,
And then swiftly by Fate's cruel "never" is crushed,
Though life's sunshine seems faded, its melody hushed,
Its gladness and sweetness forever seem o'er,
Ah, sad heart, the world sees no crape on thy door.

But think you the home whence the dear one has fled
Can lose the effulgence the spirit has shed?
Though time to eternity pass, nevermore
Can the world be again as it has been before.
So no heart can e'er measure the difference wrought
For life and for death by each dream, hope or thought.
Though thy hope never blossom or fair dream endure,
Yet know, O sad heart, that fruition is sure.

*THE TALISMAN.

Who has not read since childhood's earliest time,
In witching prose or still more witching rhyme,
The tales that swarm, like bees o'er summer flowers,
Around the old Alhambra's courts and towers?
Each carven fountain, silent now so long,
Still has its legend of enchantment strong,
And each old gateway, dungeon, vaulted hall,
Each nook and corner where the moon-beams fall
Is haunted by some story weird and old
Of the long-vanished Moorish masters told.
Enchantment holds in strange and mighty reign
The sun-kissed hills and vineyards of old Spain,
And all the sleepy land from east to west
Beneath some magic spell is said to rest.
Of these wild tales one haunts my mind to-night.
As your familiar faces greet my sight,
And, if you will, I would once more recall
The ancient legend, known, I think, to all.
'Tis this: When day's last lingering gleam is gone,
And settles down the eve of good St. John,
Then he who holds the magic charm may hear
A low deep murmur rising far and near,
And clank of armor and the steed's glad neigh,
All sounding vague and dim and far away;
And then, from mountain cavern, quiet dell,
And ruined castle, 'neath enchantment's spell,
A spectral steed and rider greet the gaze
With all the trappings of the olden days.
From all the land they haste, and e'er there falls
The hour of midnight on Granada's walls
Boabdil's glittering army waits again
As oft of old upon Granada's plain,

*Read before Alumni Association of Elyria High School.

For one short hour to fill th' Alhambra's courts
With all the ancient greetings, feasts and sports,
For ere the morning's faintest gleams appear
Each one must vanish for another year.
Ah, friends, e'en thus we meet again to-night,
And thus will vanish ere the morrow's light,
Bound by a spell almost as strong and deep
As that 'neath which the Moslem warriors sleep.
The spell of daily duty, life's demands
And toil's enchantment over brain and hands,—
We still can break, one night of all the year,
The spell that binds us, and commingle here.
But come we all?   Ah, friends, we grieve to-night
For the dear faces vanished from our sight,
For broken ranks and voices hushed to men,
Bound by a mightier power than aught we ken.
Ah, would some talisman could break the spell
That holds so fast the ones we love so well,
And grant, while moments of a night were told,
That we might meet and greet them as of old.
But only memory's talismanic hand
Hath power to bring them from the silent land:
And memory, though it bless indeed our years,
Walks never far from the dim halls of tears.
Let pass the legend, for another thought,
A weightier one, the same wierd tales have brought.
Not only through the pleasant vales of Spain
Doth strong enchantment hold a mighty reign.
The whole wide world for ages lay in sleep
Beneath a spell more potent and more deep.
And to this land and age is given to break
The magic charm and bid the nations wake.
The spell?   Ah, friends, dark ignorance alone,
The mother of all wrongs the world hath known,
All superstition, cruelty and crime
Which men have suffered since the birth of time.

I challenge you to trace one hideous thing
Which from that source of evil did not spring,
And ours the talisman to cast away
The dark enchantment and admit the day.
Nor ours alone,—how many a kindred band
The talisman holds out with eager hand!
Nor these alone—to every school-house known
Across the land as if in broadcast sown.
And slowly, slowly, for the world is wide,
The yielding fetters wi'l be cast aside
And purity and truth and right shall reign
When knowledge breaks each binding bar and chain.
For where truth reigns, reigns God, and by His will
The leaven of the truth the world shall fill.
Ah, wondrous age, and still more wondrous land,
Where lowest, highest, side by s'de may stand;
Where marble court and legislative hall
An equal welcome give to each and all;
Where birth and worth an honest balance turn,
And gold is his who hath the power to earn;
Where naught may keep the lowliest from a throne.
And kings alone by kingly deeds are known.
Aye, humble schoolroom, wheresoe'er thou art,
By country roadside or the city's heart,
Thine is the power, the talisman is thine—
The darkness yields before thy magic sign;
The sunrise brightens o'er the land and sea,
And ignorance lays down its arms to thee.
But, O my friend, though fair the dawn appear,
Think not, I pray, that more than dawn is here.
The noon-time still is far,—aye far away,—
The glorious fullness of the light of day:—
Nor will it come till, all night's banner's furled,
He comes, indeed, who "lighteth all the world."

THE BUTTERNUT BOUGH.

The butternut bough swayed over the stream;
 The stream was shallow and clear,
Darted the minnows within; without
 The dragon-fly's glittering spear.
The butternut bough, so brown and strong,
 So graceful, willowy, lithe, and long,
Drooped down so low, by the water's flow,
 We could leap and clasp it, and to and fro,
Royally swinging, the bough would go.

The butternut bough, as if nature knew
 What the farm-house children would like to do—
Nature and childhood are comrades true—
 Fashioned a seat as smooth and neat
As ever saddle for lady meet;
 Cunningly curving, safe and wide,
Waiting the children to mount and ride;
 With leafy branches for bridle and rein,
Over mountain, valley, and plain
 Galloped the charger with might and main.

Sometimes the bough was a ship, you know,
 Was there not water flowing below?
Rigging and mast and spar up there,
 Over our heads, in the summer air;
And, best of all, if a storm should wake,
 An anchor that never was known to break.
Over the sea afar sailed we,
 Ships of the king, or pirates free,
Strange and wonderful things to see.

The butternut bough swayed over the stream,
　Ah me, it was long ago,
But whether a royal carriage of state,
　Or a fiery steed or a vessel great,
Wherever we choose to go,
　Over the hill where mother and home,
As I wish they were ever for those who roam,
　Over mountain or vale or ocean-foam,
As of old on the butternut bough.

CHILDHOOD'S BIRTHRIGHT.

If our land could give to its children,
　In the first glad years of life,
A home in the beautiful country,
　Afar from the city's strife,
Away from the noise and turmoil,
　The never-ceasing tread,
The heartless struggle for riches,
　The hopeless struggle for bread,

How would the ranks be strengthened
　Of the Nation's brave and strong;
How would its records lessen
　Of poverty, crime and wrong;
For what can the city offer
　In place of forest and field?
What can its noisy pavements
　Or crowded factories yield?

For happiness cannot linger
　Where grinding poverty lives,
And the grandest home of the wealthy
　But gilded bitterness gives.

God surely meant for the children
　The strength of the mighty hills.
The richness of treasure unfailing
　Which nature's store-house fills.

O care-free days of my childhood;
　While memory holds its sway,
My heart will yield thee its homage
　Wherever my footsteps stray.
Pictures of early mornings
　Throng back from the long-ago,
When the eastern sky was flaming
　And the dew-wet grass aglow.

When up from the farthest corner
　Of the old south pasture wide
We merrily roused the cattle—
　Each with a steaming side.
Then mounting the slow farm horses
　From the old fence' top-most rail,
We drove the cows to the barnyard,
　Where waited each wide-mouthed pail.

Memories of old, old-orchards,
　Low-branching and gnarled and dim,
Of mossy northern hillsides,
　Of brooks where the minnows swim,
Of Autumn with untold treasures—
　Frost grapes luscious and sweet,
Mushrooms, and nuts half hidden
　In the gorgeous leaves at your feet.

Then let not our fair country
　Be plowed by the alien's hand.
Be proud of your farms and homesteads,
　Be proud of your fruitful land.

Know that the cities lure you
   To false and empty joys,
And thank the Lord if the country
   Can shelter your girls and boys.

GOLD.

When far from the harbor of sun-kissed Spain
The mariners sailed o'er the unknown main,
Their quest was a land of wealth untold
And their dreams were all of the shining gold.

Rich indeed was the new-found land,
Its forests boundless, its rivers grand,
Free and wonderful, wide and wild,
Beauty lavish and undefiled.

They came, and toiled, and suffered, and died,
Seeking and ever unsatisfied.
Reward abundant their labor brought,
But never the one reward they sought.

Cities arose as the time went by,
Church-spires pointed the way to the sky;
Cornfields rustled and hearth-fires gleamed,
But they found not the gold of which they dreamed.

And ever as up from the ocean wide,
Farther and farther creeps the tide.
So over the broad land day by day,
A nation was making its onward way.

Mighty rivers were curbed and spanned,
Prairies yielded their harvests grand,
Dreary deserts their secrets told,
Hills were stripped of their forests old.

And at length, when the years had come and fled
Till the tale of the whole wide land was read,
Where the sun dips into the ocean vast,
They found the wonderful gold at last.

There are torrents to cross on the path of life;
There are mountains and deserts with danger rife,
Hast thou placed, O Father, to draw us o'er,
The gold of life on the farther shore?

———

THE SONG OF YOUTH.

Youth's meadows are green beneath our feet,
Round us the summer air floats sweet,
Glimpses of hills afar to the right
Through the bending tree-tops reach our sight:
And the butterflies lazily floating by
Are not more free than you and I.

What do we care though the sages say
That summer-time cannot last alway?
Are we not standing amid youth's flowers,
With the heritage of the ages ours?
Men have been sowing through years gone by;
We are the reapers—you and I.

Poets and artists for fame have sought;
We are the future for which they wrought;
Rich is the fruitage that waits our hand;
Life and love at our bidding stand;
The treasures of earth in our pathway lie,
We will enjoy them—you and I.

Fate is a myth and youth is strong;
Life is worth living, if short or long;
Sceptre and crown we may take at will;
Thrones are waiting for us to fill.
Let us arise ere our days pass by,
Heirs of Humanity—you and I.

OHIO ALL THE YEAR.

I've thought the matter over,
　An', nigh as I kin see,
I don't know of another place
　I'd any ruther be.
The story-writers slight us,
　The poets pass us by,
But right here in Ohio
　I'd choose to live an' die.

It's just as old as Egypt,
　An' a hundred times as good;
Lake Erie's bin here longer
　Than the Pyramids hev stood,
An' if it's brains thet's wanted,
　I guess 'twould stan' a show,
Alongside any other place
　No matter whar you go.

Ohio in the spring time,
　When the apple orchards blow,
An' the cherry trees resemble
　A good-sized drift o' snow.
Ohio in the summer,
　With a thousand wheat-fields white,
When the reapers buzz by daytime,
　An' the Katydids by night—

Ohio in the autumn,
　With the robin's good-bye song—
Thanksgivin' time an' Christmas
　A'comin' right along;
Ohio in the winter,
　With the cross-roads drifted high·-
Just listen to the music
　Of the sleigh-bells jinglin' by.

With the apples an' the cider,
　In the evenin' by the blaze,
When a neighbor calls to talk about
　The Senate's cur'us ways—
Yes, lookin' at it all aroun'
　I'm willin' fer to say
I'll take, fer solid comfort,
　Ohio any day.

———

THE BROOK WHERE WE USED TO FISH.

Though many the miles that lie between
This page and that well-remembered scene,
And many the years that intervene,
Yet still I can never forget, I ween,
　The brook where we used to fi-h.

The trees arched over it, green and high,
Veiling the blue of the summer sky,
And dropping flickering shades to lie
Over the minnows swift and shy
　In the brook where we used to fish.

The banks were tunneled with muskrat holes—
Mysterious places to probe with poles—
The stones were green with the cool moss folds,
And lichens grew on the great tree-boles
　By the brook where we used to fish.

Black-snakes coiled on the sunk logs near,
Snapping-turtles and crabs were here;
But never a thought had we of fear—
Their citizenship was proved and clear
   By the brook where we used to fish.

We sat on the grassy bank in a row,—
Barefoot urchins with heads of tow,
Watching the corks float to and fro,
And the sunfish glistening down below
   In the brook where we used to fish.

Sometimes we followed its winding way
Past the butternut trees and the willows gray,
Clear to the little white bridge that lay
At the edge of the strange land stretching away
   From the brook where we used to fish.

Many a lesson, good or ill,
Many a task for heart and will
Strive the hastening years to fill,
But a scene that memory holdeth still
   Is the brook where we used to fish.

OUT OF PRISON.

Solomon, cynic, seer and sage,
Wisest of mortals in any age,
Wrote when the years had dimmed his eyes:—
"Better a child who is poor and wise;
Seeking guidance from each and all,
Than he who is born in a palace hall."

For the child from prison cometh to reign,
Slowly but surely his throne to gain;
Born to the purple, born to hear
"Vive le Roi!" with conscious ear,
Born the scepter of power to sway—
Each in his own appointed way.

Born to the purple—yes, but stay!
The royal garment is far away;
Far away, while before his eyes
The prison walls of poverty rise.
Ah, many the prince those walls restrain,
But "out of prison he cometh to reign."

Hard is the struggle those walls to scale,
But the scepter waiteth, he must not fail.
Weary the climbing, and few can see
In the humble climber the king to be.
So many the toilers, the crown so far,
What careth the world who its princes are?

Better a child who is poor and wise
Than the haughtiest form in kingly guise;
For the monarch no counsel will heed or hear;
The child is waiting with list'ning ear.
Born to the purple, indeed, but none
The crown may wear till the crown is won,

Few the kings in this land of ours
But have looked through poverty's prison bars.
Toil-marked the hands which the scepter bear,
Weary the brows which the crowns do wear.
The poor and wise have the world to gain
And "out of prison he cometh to reign."

IN THE LIBRARY.

Over the green-robed hills away
To the ebb tide sand fields stretching gray,
Over the opal tinted spray
Hide and seek 'mongst the rocks at play,
    Over the ocean prairies,—
Away, away and still away,
Time and distance—naught are they;
Bring tomorrow what it may,
All the earth is mine today,
    Mine the wings of fairies.

Kings and queens in rich array
At my bidding, go or stay,
Castle-towers and gardens gay,--
Forests where shy deer stray;
    All the Orient's treasures,—
Gilded mosques where Moslems pray,
Cities by the Persian Bay,
Where the vales enchanted lay;
Who hath power to say me nay?
    Mine the wide world's pleasure.

WHEN SHADOWS FALL.

When shadows fall and birds chirp low,
    When homeward weary toilers go,
When beetles wheel and daisies close,
    When play-worn children seek repose,
Then let sweet thoughts arise in all,
    When shadows fall, when shadows fall.

When shadows fall, and clear and far,
    Shines in the sky the evening star,
Then be all bitterness forgot,
    All blinding hatred flourish not,
Peace on the heart's high throne install
    When shadows fall, when shadows fall.

When shadows fall and work doth cease,
    Bid worldly cares thy soul release;
Let charity and love arise
    As darkness softly veils the skies;
Then sweet shall be life's vesper call,
    When shadows fall, when shadows fall.

"TILL DEATH US JOIN."

A grave-yard lies in the city's heart,
    High-walled and aged and gray,
A place from the city's noise apart,
    Closed book of a by-gone day.

Thick lies the graves with their sunken stones,
    And the hand of Time—ah me!—
Has almost hidden the legends quaint
    With its mossy tracery.

One grave is close by a dying elm,
    And the traveler there may see:
"To Samuel, aged twenty-four,
    Died eighteen thirty-three."

And away, ah! far away to-night
    Where the fire-light fades and glows
A woman sits: On her thin hair white
    More than eighty winters' snows.

And ever the name in her busy thoughts,
    The name that she whispers low,
Is Samuel, love of her girlhood days,
    The husband of long ago.

Vanished the present, and hers once more
    The past with its hopes and fears.
The brave boy husband again is hers,
    Though dust for these sixty years.

Another has called her wife since then:
    The heads of her sons are gray;
But not of them is her thought or speech
    As fadeth her life's long day.

Her name again is the name he gave;
    His ring on her worn hand gleams.
Of him are ever the tales she tells,
    Of him are her happy dreams.

On, Samuel, aged twenty-four,
    Boy-husband, lover and friend,
No grave over thee has victory,
    Love knoweth no bound or end.

To her thy hair is as brown to-night—
    As tender thy voice and low
As when you loved her, your fair girl-bride,
    Full seventy years ago.

ASLEEP.

Low 'mid the downy pillows
    Brown curls and rings of gold;
The baby's dimpled fingers
    The Mother's gently fold.
Soft cheek 'gainst soft cheek resting
    While evening shadows creep,
White lids the brown eyes veiling,
    Mother and babe,—asleep.

      He bent to watch them, smiling,
        Tears gleaming through the smile,
      And words of prayer, unbidden,
        Rose silently the while.

Still 'mid the snowy blossoms
    Brown curls and rings of gold:
The baby's waxen fingers
    Again the Mother's fold.
No bloom the cold cheeks tinting
    No breathings soft and deep
Brown eyes no more to open—
    Mother and babe,—asleep.

      He stood beside them silent.
        No moan, no tear, no prayer.
      Joy drains the heart's deep fountains,
        Grief finds but dark despair.

THE PASSING OF DAWN.

Across the prairie breaks the dim, sweet morn;
  With low, glad rustle wakes the serried corn;
The tiny, timid things housed underground
  Dawn's subtile perfume brings to list the sound,
And all the air with rapture throbs and swells
  The soul-heard music of Dawn's thousand bells.

The floating rose-leaves in the Eastern sky
  Are born in sheaves by opal waves on high,
While in the West the ashes of the night
  Beyond our quest are swept by fingers white.
Dawn's feet afar the mountain-tops have trod;
  Oh hearts of men, awake,—to work—and God.

SONG.—DO THEY WHISPER.

Blossoms and buds of the springtime,
  Ringing your dainty-sweet bells,
What are the fairy-land stories
  Your dim-chiming melody tells?
What do the soft breezes whisper?
  What do the butterflies say!
What do the dew-jewels murmur
  As into the shadows you sway?
Do they whisper, "We love you, we love you,"
  Through all of the long happy day?

AMBITION.

He who Pegasus would conquer, long and
    lonely must he ride:
Toil and weariness await him who
    would climb Parnassus' side.
In the valley is contentment, pleasant
    rest and loving friend;
On the heights are cold and hunger,
    pain and longing without end.
What if glory bathe the summit, 'tis but
    sunlight on the snow,—
Dreary wind that ceases never,—warmth
    and verdure lie below.

RETROSPECTION.

Across the lapse of years which seem
Like the frail fabric of a dream,
The full, fair yesterdays of youth
Gaze at me with their eyes of truth,
And say, with voice that clearer grows
As wax and wane life's suns and snows:
"Oh toiler, dreamer, weary-eyed,
Drop your thorn-woven robes of pride,
So cold, so harsh, so dearly bought;
Your crowns with glistening tears inwrought;—
We are the real; all that you grasp
Doth fade and vanish from your clasp.
Earth's gifts are all alike in this—
Possession brings not happiness:
Pleasure and bitterness are one;
Ambition's task is never done,

And, like the rainbow's pot of gold,
Success ye seek but never hold.
We are the real; your childhood years,
Undimmed by time, unstained by tears;
What know we of the pride of birth?
What know we of the rank of earth?
Deceit or vanity or pain,
The fight for bread, the lust of gain?
Come back to us; the keys we hold
Which open gates to streets of gold.
Though twice a thousand years have fled
Re-echo still the words He said—
To breathe the air of Heaven mild
You must be as a little child."

O Beckoning youth! I would the way
Were shorter and the sky less gray.
I would the path, so hard to climb,
Could be retraced to thy dear time;
I would the scars on heart and brain
Some kind hand could erase again,
Brush off the dust of toil and sin,
And let the light of childhood in.
And Thou, Our Father, high above
Our blindest wanderings, in Thy love
O lead us, though we cannot see,
To childhood's purity, and Thee.

WITH MEMORY'S EYES.

Ah, sing not of Italian skies,
   Of English moors and meadows,
Of torrents dark whose gleam and spark
   Leap down 'mid Alpine shadows;

For, wander wheresoe'er you will,
  The heart of each turns gladly still
To unsung grove and unsought rill
  That knew your childhood's hours.

No brighter skies have ever shone
  Than those your childhood days have known,
And never bloomed in any zone
  Aught fairer buds and flowers.

Then scorn not your familiar fields,
  Dream not of castles olden,
For comes the day when you shall say
  The scenes of youth are golden.

———

DAWN.

Dun smoke upcurling to a roseate sky
  From gray-walled cots with eastern windows flaming,
A frost touched land: A rose-gray symphony
  The new-born day with tender touch proclaiming.

———

SINCE THOU ART AWAY.

Since thou art away
All our joys go astray,
And fadeth each blossom and vine.
The trees sigh in grief
And low droppeth each leaf
And the stars have forgotten to shine.

Since thou art away
The soft Moon will not stay,
And fled is her radiance divine.
The sea weepeth soft,
And the birds grieve aloft,
And the stars have forgotten to shine.

Since thou art away
When the sweet breezes play
The name that they whisper is thine;
And the night and the day
Sad and slow pass away
And the stars have forgotten to shine.

A PORTENT.

O'er Southern seas that Autumn night
Uncounted stars shed shimmering light
And blue depths mirrored back the sight
A thousand years the same.
For never sea or sky had known
The echoes of a human tone
Or stars on human form had shone
With radiant tropic flame.

But Fate upon the page of Time
That night had marked with touch sublime
To shape each future age and clime
And perish nevermore.
For ships with tapering spar and mast
Black shadows on the waters cast
And broke the ripples as they passed
To seek an unknown shore.

Through weary months the sun's last ray
Had tinged their prows at close of day
And still their course unchanging lay—
    Westward turned every eye.
And now on one high deck there stands
A man whose tireless vision scans
For fleeting outlines of fair lands
    The circle of the sky.

Columbus! Worthy of the name!
Christ-bearer,—Christopher,—he came
Seeking not merely wealth or fame
    But lead by purpose high;
And now as draws the moment near
To prove his wondrous vision clear
What Fate-fraught signal shall appear
    To greet the Leader's eye?

Listen, Oh Country of the Free,
Listen, Oh lands beyond the sea,
Listen, Oh Nations yet to be!
    What met the Master's sight?
A prophesy it was indeed,
A message for the world to read,
A lesson for all Time to heed,—
    The shining of a light.

And thou,—hast thou fulfilled, Oh Land,
Thy destiny God-willed and grand,
A light within the world to stand?
    Thou hast, fair land of mine.
A light to freedom for all men,
For heart and hand, for voice and pen;
A light to show to mortal ken
    Man's liberty divine.

A light to home and womanhood,
To greatest growth and highest good,
Equality and brotherhood
    For each and all the same.
Oh Land, of all the ages heir,
Send out thy radiance broad and fair
That all within the earth may share
    Thy truth-revealing flame.

SWALLOWS.

To-day the swallows flying
    Through Summer air o'erhead
Bring visions to my fancy
    From years forever fled.
I see a low-browed homestead,
    'Neath drooping Maple leaves,
And near it stands an old red barn
    With swallows round the eaves.

Refrain.

Oh swallows, swallows, swallows,
    Ye bear my heart away
To other climes and other scenes,
    Now flown for many a day.

The shadows all are length'ning
    From out the flaming West
And circling. circling downward
    The swallows seek their nest
A Mother's voice is calling,
    The cattle homeward go,
And hidden 'neath the old barn eaves
    The swallows twitter low.

Refrain.

Oh swallows, swallows, swallows,
Ye bear my heart away
To other climes and other scenes,
Now flown for many a day.

NELLIE.

Nellie stands at the molding-board
Touched by the warm sunlight
Her sleeves to her dainty elbows rolled
Her arms all dimpled and white.
She hums a tune as she works away,
"Douglas tender and true;"
Oh Nellie, my thoughts with the flour you sift,
And every thought is of you.

Nellie stands at the moulding-board,—
Dreamy her downcast face;
Her pink-tipped fingers in and out
Glance with a witching grace
Nod and quiver the tiny curls
Crowning her girlish head,—
Oh Nellie, Nellie, you knead my heart
In with your loaves of bread.

Nellie, there in your cotton gown
Simple and fresh and neat,
Flour on your fingers fit for gems
Earnest your eyes and sweet,
Shaping your snowy loaves with care,
Ne'er was a fairer sight:
My heart will be light as the bread you knead
If you'll tell me "yes" to-night.

A VISION.

A dream of Death and a dream of Bliss
A dream of the Life that circles this,
    A dream of the endless day.
A dream of barriers cast aside,—
Of gates to Infinity opened wide,—
    Of Mortality passed away.

We had left the bondage of work and tears
Of darkness and sorrow, of failure and fears,—
And stood where Eternity's dawning clears
    From the midnight of time at last.
We knew as a day a thousand years
    And a thousand days had passed.

In the lap of the Universe lay impearled
The atom we erst had called the World,
    Its part in the Infinite done.
The scroll of the Lord to our sight unrolled
And we traced through its workings fold by fold
    The plan of the Mighty One.

We saw, as we deem the angels do,
The near and distant, the false and true,
    With God-born, limitless sight;
And the great life-principle shut in our soul
Felt the fetters away from its memory roll
    And it wakened again to light.

We knew the cycles ere Time had birth,—
Ere the voice of the Lord brought forth the Earth,
    As yesterdays after sleep.
And the ages of men before us rolled,
The Nations of earth in graves long cold,
    Through centuries buried deep.

    *   *   *   *   *   *

And wherever mortals lived and died,
Walking among them side by side,
    Brothers in toil and pain,
Where those whom the Lord had drawn apart
Nearer the pulse of the mighty heart
    Freer from earthly stain.

They saw, the Finite piercing through,
Things fairer than their brothers knew,
    Heights nearer to the sun;
And heard, above Earth's myriad cries,
Faint echoings from beyond the skies;
    And dreamed of victories won.

They caught, from earth and sea and air,
God's beauty, spreading everywhere,
    And prisoned it in song;
And bound in columned beatings deep
The strains that through the ages sweep
    With pulsings solemn, strong.

They felt the crown of kingship weigh
Their weary brows whereon it lay
    Yet joyfully they sang.
Earths bitterness and pain and woe
Full deeply did their spirits know,
And in their music's changing flow
    The tones of sorrow rang.

They let the ties of Heaven bind
Their hearts to hearts of all mankind
    In mighty brotherhood,
And lived to point each fettered soul
On toward the God-appointed goal
    Of the Eternal Good.

Then to our minds in vision rose
The laurel-circled brows of those
    Whom we in life had known.
We called them Poets. Manifold
In latter days and days of old
    They sang in varied tone.

The voice that told the wondrous fall
Of angel throngs from Heaven's wall,
    With solemn rhythm deep.
And his who trod with bended head,
By Rome's supremest singer led
    Where Pluto's shadows sweep.

And that one whom the Master sent—
A Poet and a Mother blent—
Whose heart of womanhood was rent
    By toiling children's moan.
She who could look for brother's sake,
Beyond her pain-spent life and make
    A nation's grief her own.

And all who sang, in simpler lays,
Their songs of life and love and praise,
    Of labor and of rest.
Who gladdened weary heart and brain,
Or lightened life's abiding pain,
    While earth their footsteps pressed.

And we, e'en there, in rev'rence bent
To those rare souls which Heaven sent
    To bless the earth with song.
Who gave to man their best of life,
Who showed the victory after strife,—
    The crowning of the strong.

THE WHITE MAN'S PRIVILEGE.

"Take up the White Man's burden;"
  Two lands the strains repeat,
They echo through our musings,
  And on our heart strings beat.
"Take up the White Man's burden;"
  Our greatest poet sings;
And yet, amid the music,
  A note of discord rings.

"Take up the White Man's burden;"
  Oh God, is this our thought?
Can this be all the lesson
  Our liberty has taught?
Nay, looking o'er the oceans,
  We face the waiting world,
And give them back their answer,
  Like Sinai's thunder's hurled.

We take the White Man's privilege,
  As heirs come to their own;
As kings take up the sceptre,
  And seek the waiting throne.
We take the White Man's privilege
  With courage and with prayer,
Put childish things behind us,
  And ask for strength to dare.

We take the White Man's privilege.
  The legacy of work
The Son of God bequeathed us,
  Which none who serve may shirk.
He bore the self-same burden.
  Up Calvary's fearful side;
For thankless ones He suffered
  For those who jeered, He died.

We take the White Man's privilege,
 The un-taught ones to teach;
The wild and sullen peoples,
 To seek for and to reach.
We give our best and noblest,
 Our best is none too good;
We seek not thanks or payment,
 But only brotherhood.

We take the White Man's privilege;
 With saints and martyr's share,
To raise the ones who perish;
 To give our toil and care.
To turn the dark world slowly
 But surely toward the light;
The sunbeams of God's message,
 To flash across its night.

What though they weigh and judge us;
 What though they spurn our care,
And smite the hand that lifts them,
 And mock the pleading prayer?
There rises to our vision,
 A cross—a rock hewn tomb,
An Angel guarded doorway,
 A voice that pierced the gloom.

We take the White Man's privilege;
 Our God who sits on high,
Has opened wide the pathway,
 We can but do or die.
No more to stand safe-shielded,
 While others lead the fray;
Our hour has struck. We answer;
 We come, Oh Earth, to-day.

THE HEIGHT AND THE VALLEY.

A child at play in the grass and clover
  Finds a pebble the rain washed clear,
A feather dropped when the doves flew over
  Or the blue of a robin-egg's glistening sphere.
Ah, mother, bearing to thee her treasure,
  Soft hair flying and eyes agleam,
She cannot know in her childish pleasure
  How small to thee does the treasure seem.

She lays it away with her dimpled fingers
  Safe with the things she holds most dear,
And the little box where the treasure lingers,
  Adds to its prizes year by year;
A curl of gold from her girl-friend's tresses;
  The girl whom the angels found so soon—
Pieces cut from her dainty dresses
  When her life was bright as the days of June.

Flowers that he brought, her first boy-lover,
  Careless of eye and fair of face;
And flowers again, with the touch of another
  Lending their beauty deeper grace.
Ah, naught on earth or the heaven above her
  Seemed to the maid so fair, so dear,
As the joyous face of her girlhood's lover,
  As the ringing voice so free and clear.

Pass the years and a woman. kneeling —
  Thick in her hair the threads of snow —
Gazes into a box revealing
  Faded relics of long ago.

Smiles she sad at the sometime treasures.
   Flowers of the lover and child's delight,
Harvest of longings, hopes and pleasures
   Worthless alike to the wider sight.

O Father, Father, who changest never,
   Is it all so small that we long for here?
Is naught on earth worth the striving after
   When the strife is past and the vision clear?
Earth's honors, gold and fame and learning
   Which our hands so often raise on high,
Are our prizes small to Thy discerning
   As the childish prize to the older eye?

THE END.